TABLE OF CONTENTS

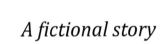

A fictional story

*~To my parents, who have shown me
what it means to be loved~*

*~And for the glory of my King, who died
so that I could be adopted as His Princess ~*

ACKNOWLEDGMENTS:

Thank you to my late grandmother, BabaAnne. You inspired me to write, and because of your generosity, I was able to publish my first book. I look forward to seeing you again in Heaven!

My sister, Ceyda, who is my own personal cheerleader, and who brings laughter and joy to everything we do together. God has given you amazing talents and I am excited to see how He leads you to use them for His glory!

Thank you, Mama and Daddy, for always believing in me, encouraging me, loving me and training me. I love you!!

Many thanks to my good friends, who helped me edit this book and offered their encouragement and prayers: Bethany and Zachoia Cooper, Sabrina and Amanda Hubbard, Jill Petipas, Haven Sidell and Abigail Smith. You are all such a blessing to me!

Thank you to Xulon Press for their fantastic service and support!

CHAPTER ONE

I stood alone, all alone. Even though I was surrounded by people milling about, I couldn't help feeling alone. I now had the full Atlantic Ocean between me and him. I stayed at the landing pad for a while, breathing in the fresh air and taking in my surroundings. I looked for any bit of France in what I could see of Boston, Massachusetts. Tall skyscrapers reached up into the clouds. People were everywhere; bumping, jostling, talking and shouting. The baby that had cried the whole plane ride now emerged from the aircraft cradled in its mother's arms. An old pain stabbed at my heart as I watched them walk past me and meet a man who appeared to be the father. He kissed the mother and tickled the baby under her chin. I watched, sadly, mesmerized, fighting back tears.

"Excuse me, Miss?" I turned around to see a flight attendant loaded down with suitcases, looking down at me quizzically.

"Yes sir," I whispered, clumsily stepping out of the way while digging in my pocket for the slip of paper that the supervisor had given to me before I had boarded the airplane back in France. I glanced up, searching the crowds for the little family, but they were gone. "*Just like my dreams,*" I thought miserably.

The slip of paper said to go into the big building and follow the signs to the customs desk. I began walking, dragging my single suitcase behind me. I was supposed to look for Mr. and Mrs. Budd. A picture of the supervisor's stern face flashed through my mind.

"Don't be gloomy. What's wrong with you? You're being adopted! You're one of the lucky ones," he had lectured me while we were waiting at the airport in France.

I shivered, thinking how the *unlucky* ones were feeling right now. I would not soon be missing the dreary, dirty, hopeless group home with its peeling paint and sad faces that I had just come from. I referred to it as 'My Orphanage,' even though it really was a temporary place for kids who were in between foster homes. Foster kids and orphans in France were usually quickly taken in or adopted by family members or citizens of France. However, I was different. I didn't have any family members who would take me in. They all remembered my parents' past and weren't willing to be associated with it. No one else wanted me, even though I knew the social workers really were trying to get me off their hands. I suppose the government just couldn't figure out what to do with me. I went through two horrid foster homes before landing the group home, which acted as a permanent foster home for orphans who had nowhere else to go. Since the inter-country adoption process was so long and complicated that very few people wanted to go through it, orphans who were stuck in these situations were pretty much doomed for the rest of their miserable lives.

Still, even in this dreary setting, I had been able to hold onto one piece of comfort. I had always wished—I had always hoped—that he would come back for me. I had imagined the scene over and over again when I needed to comfort myself. Father would come jollily into my orphanage, bringing beams of sunlight with him. "Where's my little Princess?" He would ask. I would run into his arms and he would pick me up and twirl me around. We would laugh together and he would bring me home with him. It seemed so real, I had almost convinced myself it was going to happen. *"Any day now,"* I would whisper to myself when I was alone in the dark at night. *"Any day it's going to happen. And I'll be going home."*

But I couldn't keep imagining anymore. Now I was in America, with nothing but a suitcase, a folder full of papers, and a broken heart. Reality blew over me like the icy wind and rain when you open a door in the Arctic, hitting you so hard it takes your breath away. Now I knew what I should have known all along: my dream was gone. I had to admit that I couldn't keep deceiving myself by thinking that things would go back as they had—or should have—been. A tear fell onto the paper I held in my hand, blurring the letters. I sniffled back my emotions and walked briskly into the building.

The airport was crowded. I had to stand in a long line as I made my way through customs, and wait for a heavyset man in a uniform to review my papers. Finally emerging from the customs area after 30 minutes, I froze when daylight struck me square in the face. Dazed, I blinked as I let my eyes become adjusted to the lighting. I had entered a huge hall with glass walls, which was the baggage claim area. I took a deep breath and turned as I let my gaze sweep across the terminal. It was filled to the brim with people. Some were waiting to meet their friends or family, some were standing with their luggage, and everyone was coming and going. It was dizzying to try and discern one from another. There was so much happening all at once. As I stood there self-consciously, I observed many happy reunions taking place between parties. My eyes timidly combed the crowd, looking for a friendly face with whom I might belong. I felt out of place and clumsy, like the whole world was staring at me and saying, "You don't belong here! Go back to where you belong!"

As much as I wanted to, though, I couldn't go back. I was stuck here now, trapped like a mosquito in a spider's web. And I didn't belong. Feelings of despair and frustration rose in my throat. I knew

I was going to cry. I felt like bolting back outside, back on the plane that would take me home.

My wandering eyes suddenly landed upon a kind looking lady and a man with two little boys standing right across from me, hemmed in by other people. Our gazes met. I saw her lean towards the man and point at a photograph that the she held in her hand, then look up at me again. She began to walk across the terminal towards me.

"Are you Saranna?" she asked. Her voice was sweet and kind. I stared at her, nodding numbly.

She wrapped her arms around me and hugged me. I can't remember the last time someone hugged me. She smelled sweet and her body felt soft and comforting against mine. I melted into her arms and laid my head on her shoulder. I couldn't hold it back any longer. My throat burned from holding it all in. My heart cracked and tears began to fall on the woman's pretty turquoise sweater. Is this what it felt like to have a real mother who loves you? I cried. I cried for the mother I never knew, for the father I lost, and for the memories I never made.

The lady pulled back and brushed my matted hair out of my wet face. "My, you look just as pretty as I imagined you," she almost whispered. I could see that her own eyes were glistening with tears, yet a smile took up her whole face. Her smile looked just like I'd pictured my Mother's to be. Black curls reached down to her shoulders and framed her round face. She was beautiful. Could she really think that I was pretty? I smiled a watery smile through my tears.

"I'm Alicia Budd," she introduced herself. Turning to the small group waiting behind her, she continued, "And this is my husband, Clark. And this is Matthew and Titus," she said, pointing to the two little blond haired, wide eyed boys, who half hid behind their father. Mr. Budd was tall and had short, blond-orange hair. "Hello there," he said cordially, as he stepped closer. His voice was soft and deep. "Boys, say 'Hi' to Saranna," he instructed kindly. "Hi," they both whispered together to me.

Mrs. Budd laughed. "These boys have been so excited to meet you! We've all been praying for you since about two years ago, before we even knew your name."

I was awestruck. These people were so warm and kind. For some reason, I suppose when I thought about new parents or even grown-ups, I thought of the foster families that I had been in. But this family actually cared enough to be praying for me. I could not fathom praying for someone I didn't even know. Had their prayers really made a difference? Is that why I was here?

"You get to see our room!" one of the boys burst out. I think it was Titus.

"But you get to have your own room," said the other. Matthew must have been a bit older than his brother because he was a little taller. Aside from that, they looked identical.

"Let's all go to the car and we can talk more about it," said Mr. Budd. Together as a group, we retrieved my suitcase from the baggage carousel. Then Mrs. Budd gathered up Titus and we all followed Mr. Budd out the door of the terminal. Matthew smiled up at me and fell into step beside me, occasionally interrupting his gait to add in a little joyful skip. Instinctively, I held his hand while crossing the parking lot.

Mr. Budd unlocked a dark green mini-van and loaded my suitcase into the trunk. Mrs. Budd buckled in the boys while I stood by watching.

"Why don't you sit in the back between the boys?" Mrs. Budd smiled at me. "They both wanted to sit next to you today."

"How old are you?" Matthew asked as Mr. Budd started the car.

I glanced at Mrs. Budd before I answered. "Thirteen," I said.

"Wow," responded Titus. "I'm only four." He tried to hold up all four of his small fingers.

"I'm five," said Matthew proudly. "And I'm almost six."

"That's right," said Mr. Budd. "In exactly two months." He smiled at Matthew in the rearview mirror, and Matthew glowed.

"When is your birthday?" Titus asked quizzically.

"I don't know," I answered quietly. "We didn't have birthdays at the group home. We just all became a year older in January."

Poor Titus looked confused. Matthew did, too. An awkward silence followed.

"So you never had cake, or ice cream, or presents?" Matthew asked, his voice rising in disbelief at the injustice.

I shrugged, feeling bad I had mentioned anything about it. That was the only way I had ever remembered it, so I didn't really think much of it now.

"Boys," suggested Mr. Budd, changing the subject, "tell Saranna about your dinosaurs."

A lively conversation on the boys' part continued for the next hour that we were in the car. I started to wonder what it would be like living with this new family.

CHAPTER TWO

"Here we are," said Mrs. Budd as the car pulled into a driveway.

I looked out the window. A pretty brown house with tan shutters sat amidst tall evergreen trees in the middle of a lawn, still patched with brown from enduring a long winter. Tulips popped up out of the ground along the driveway, and a swing set stood in the far corner of the yard. Mrs. Budd came around the back and helped unbuckle the boys while I hopped out on my own. Mr. Budd got my suitcase out of the trunk and led the way up the concrete steps to the front door. Upon opening it, I stepped into a large room with couches and an easy chair along the walls. A coffee table with picture frames sat in the middle of the room, and a bookcase stood against the wall. Through another doorway I could see what looked like a kitchen, and behind two glass sliding doors was a deck. To our right was a set of stairs.

"I'll show you your room," said Mrs. Budd, walking upstairs. I took my suitcase and followed her.

At the top of the stairs, we walked down a hallway lined with several doors. At the end of the hallway, I stood at the open doorway of my room, almost afraid to go in. It was beautiful. The walls were painted soft purple and a cozy tan area rug covered the floor. White muslin curtains hung before an open window, billowing in the breeze. A bed with a light-colored quilt coverlet stood in the middle of the room, and above the bed was a frame with the words, "Jesus Christ is the same yesterday, today, and forever" embroidered in it.

I felt like a real princess in her chamber. Remembering how my father used to call me "My Little Princess" brought tears to my eyes all over again. I walked into the room and impatiently wiped them away, not wanting to let Mrs. Budd see.

Mrs. Budd stood in the doorway watching me. "Are you okay?" she asked.

I nodded quickly.

"Do you want me to stay and help you unpack your things?"

I didn't know if I wanted her to stay or leave. Eventually I shook my head. "I can do it. Thanks."

Mrs. Budd smiled at me and walked down the hallway.

I sighed and looked around again. A white dresser sat on the opposite side of the room, and a desk with a chair was set up in the corner. A sliding closet door opened to the right of the bedroom door. The name "Saranna" was printed in fancy letters above it. I sat down on the bed. It felt soft and comforting. Frilly white pillows sat against the headboard. I looked over and saw that on the nightstand next to my bed, underneath the lamp, sat a book. It was a large book, bound with a black leather cover. A note was propped up next to it. It read,

"*Saranna -*
Jesus loves you."

A breeze rippled through the room and made the curtains billow again. It bathed my hot face in its cooling sensation.

"Daddy, where are you?" I whispered to the air. I laid down on the bed and cried.

It was near six o'clock when Mrs. Budd called upstairs saying that supper was ready. I walked downstairs to the kitchen and took a seat at a round wooden table. A steaming pot of soup was in the center and each place was set with a bowl, spoon, napkin and glass. A plate of warm bread and a dish of yellow butter were also set on the table. The boys came scampering in and scrambled for a chair next to me. Mr. and Mrs. Budd smiled at each other and sat across from me.

"Let's pray," said Mr. Budd, bowing his head. Mrs. Budd and the boys followed suit.

Uncomfortably, I looked down at my bowl, unable to keep myself from glancing up throughout the prayer.

"Our Heavenly father, we thank You for this meal that You have provided for us. We thank You that Saranna is finally here with us, and we pray that she would feel at home. Please bless this food, and bless our family to Your service. Amen."

Everyone looked up. Mrs. Budd began filling bowls with soup and passing them around.

"Saranna, would you like some soup?"

"Yes please," I answered politely.

"Have you ever been to school?" she asked as she filled my bowl and passed it back to me.

I had to think about that one. I had gone to school with my foster families, but I hadn't officially gone to school while in my orphanage.

"I went for probably a little more than a year during 3rd grade, but I didn't make it through 4th. We studied at the group home, but I don't think I ever got past the 5th grade there."

Mr. Budd put in comfortingly, "You don't have to worry about what grade you're in. We homeschool, so you can learn at your own level. If you need to catch up, that'll happen quickly."

Mrs. Budd nodded. "In a couple weeks is registration for our homeschool co-op. On Friday mornings a bunch of homeschooling families get together at a church. The moms offer classes, and you can choose which classes you would like to be in."

I didn't often give much thought to school, and I didn't know if I liked it or dreaded it. School was the only time that I could get away from my foster families during the weeks that I had lived with them, but a lot of the kids were mean to me and the teachers always yelled at me. I could never finish my homework, so I got failing grades the whole way through.

That's why I never really made it through fifth grade. The homeschool co-op sounded strange. I had never heard of homeschooling, although I guess that is more or less what we did at my orphanage. Each person was responsible to get their own assignments done in the "School Hour" which was from 2 o'clock through 4 o'clock. We had studied subjects such as math, science, and English, yet it was always boring and monotonous. I wondered if this homeschool co-op would be different.

"All the people are very nice and the classes are really interesting," said Mrs. Budd, as if reading my thoughts. "Plus, you can choose which three classes you want to take." She smiled. "We want to make learning fun, and it's easier to have more flexibility when you homeschool."

I tried to smile back at her. I really was grateful for her efforts to make me feel at home. I had so many feelings bottled up inside, though, that I wasn't sure what to think anymore. In a way, I felt miserable. I had so many nice things now, but I was so confused and upset that I didn't think I deserved any of them. I felt almost like a betrayer when I thought of the Budd family as my family, knowing that my own father and maybe even my mother were still alive back in France. I don't know why they had to take him away from me.

Later that night, when I was tucked snugly into bed under clean sheets and the warm quilt, the only light showing through the window was a half-moon. It reflected off the wall and landed on the book that was still sitting on my nightstand. I could just barely make out the letters on the note that was propped against it, but I knew what it said. *"Jesus loves you."* My mind wandered and I remembered what Mr. Budd had said for prayers at the dinner table: *"...Our Heavenly Father..."* The phrase echoed around and around in my head as I drifted off to sleep. What did it mean? Who was this Heavenly Father? How could I possibly have three fathers and be loyal to them all? *"Jesus loves you..."* How could Jesus love me? I didn't know him, so how could he know me? I felt sleepy as all these questions crowded my mind. I saw the phrase on paper and heard Mr. Budd's soft voice say it again and again. *"Jesus loves you"...."Our Heavenly Father..."*

I woke up at 1:38 am. I couldn't fall back asleep. Jet lag had really taken its toll on me. I tossed this way and that way. The coverlet became hot, so I threw it down at the foot of the bed. I sat up and walked toward the window. The June wind played with my hair. I knelt down and rested my elbow on the windowsill. The moon was dangling over the horizon. It would be another couple hours before the sky began to get light. I breathed in the fresh night air, and then blew it out again. What was I doing here? I squinted at the clock and counted the hours. It would be about 7:30 am in France right now. I imagined all the kids in my orphanage doing their chores, still tired from waking at 5 am. I remembered that it was only 36 hours ago when I was doing the same thing. I imagined with disgust my foster families just waking up, and my foster siblings walking to school, jostling, joking and teasing the whole way. But then, I imagined my father waking up and looking at the sun, wondering if today would be the day that he would find his long lost daughter; His Princess. Pressure built behind my eyes, but the tears would not come—I had cried too much already, today. He didn't even know that I wasn't in France anymore!

And then a horrible thought snuck its way into my head. What if he didn't even care about me anymore? What if he wasn't looking for me? I shook my head violently as if that would chase the thought away. Of course he was looking for me! I was his Princess, right? But what if he didn't love me? What if....?

I laid my aching face on my arm. What did it matter anyway? I tried to convince myself that it didn't matter, that nothing mattered. I was good at doing that in my orphanage and the foster homes. I had just pretended that nothing was wrong and that nothing mattered to numb myself. At least then I couldn't feel the pain. But now...it was no use. I couldn't forget my father. I couldn't stop wishing. Or was it hoping? No, I figured at this point it would be wishing. There was no way that anything could come true anymore. I found myself whispering gibberish, to no one but myself, to nothing but darkness. "Nothing matters...I can deal....he loves me still...or does he even? But that doesn't matter....no, I can forget..."

I finally fell asleep on the floor under the window and didn't wake up again until sunlight pierced through my eyelids.

CHAPTER THREE

The next morning, a soft knocking on my door awakened me. I sat up sorely and rubbed my eyes before groggily calling, "Come in."

Mrs. Budd stepped in and smiled at me. "Good morning, Saranna! I just wanted to let you know that breakfast is hot downstairs. Come down when you're ready."

Mrs. Budd did a double take of me. "Did you sleep on the floor last night?"

I shrugged sheepishly.

She laughed. "Don't worry, you'll get used to your new bed soon enough." With an encouraging nod to me, she closed the door softly behind her.

I sighed, yawned, and stretched my arms up in the air, wincing as I felt my sore shoulders. I loved how Mrs. Budd had a way of making me feel at ease, even though I was sure she had no idea what my heart was really feeling.

Once I set foot at the bottom of the stairs, the aroma of cinnamon and freshly baked oatmeal greeted me from the kitchen. Titus came running to meet me, with Matthew not far behind. As I sat down at the table with a bowl of good-smelling, steaming oatmeal in front of me, the chatter of happy little boys coming from the other room, and Mrs. Budd's singing as she washed dishes, I again was reminded of how lucky I was. A pang of almost guiltiness hit me square in the chest, and for a second I couldn't swallow my food.

I decided to be on my own for most of the morning, but later that afternoon Mrs. Budd invited me to join her for the boys' history lesson. She read aloud from a book about the great general George Washington. At first, I wasn't sure how I was going to like learning with two little boys, but as Mrs. Budd began to read, I felt myself becoming more and more interested. I could sympathize with some of the soldiers of the Continental army, feeling their loneliness just like my own. I found myself inwardly cheering for the men as they marched against the British and won battles, despite all odds. Then we got to the questions and answers at the end of the chapter.

"Did George Washington rely on God for his strength? Do you think this is why he won so many battles?"

The boys enthusiastically answered, "Yes!" Matthew added passionately, "He won because God was with him!"

"What do you think, Saranna?" Mrs. Budd asked me.

I thought, *"Why would she be interested in my answer?"* The truth was I didn't really have an answer. You could clearly see that George Washington gave all the glory to his God, but couldn't all his victories have been a coincidence, as well? I didn't know. Still, Mrs. Budd was looking at me, waiting for my answer.

"I don't know," I finally said.

"Well," replied Mrs. Budd, "we know that George Washington prayed to God, and he also won battles that many thought he couldn't. There is a Bible verse that says, 'If God is for us, who can be against us?'"[1] She looked at the boys. "Can we all memorize this verse together?"

The two boys nodded and slowly repeated after her, "If God is for us, who can be against us?" Mrs. Budd nodded at me, so I joined in. After four or five times, we were all saying it mostly on our own.

"Now boys, go put your papers and pencils away and you are done with school for today." The boys whooped, jumped up, and dashed off so that I was left alone with Mrs. Budd.

"Saranna," she began slowly, "can I share something with you?" I evaluated her tone. Was I in for a lecture? She had said it sincerely, as if she really had a special secret that she wanted to share with me.

"Do you know why we adopted you?" I shook my head. She continued,

"For a long time Mr. Budd and I had wanted a family of our own, but for many painful years we

---

[1] Romans 8:31

were not able to. During that difficult season, God blessed us with two precious, little lives for a very short time before He saw fit to bring them out of this world. Even though it seemed at first that God had left us, as time went on we began to realize that He had indeed been there all along. He was lovingly and patiently waiting for us, to see if we had enough faith in Him to trust Him and praise Him despite our circumstances. We decided to put our hope in Him, not in our own desires, and we kept on going, even though we had much grief and were tempted to despair. Then God, in His perfect timing, entrusted us with the two beautiful, healthy boys that we have now."

I didn't really understand how this had anything to do with my adoption, but I could hear the pain in Mrs. Budd's voice when she talked about the babies that she had lost. I thought about losing my father. That had been hard for me, and my heart still hurt when I thought about it. I wondered if it was just as painful—or maybe even more—to lose a little baby, so fragile and sweet, whom you were responsible for bringing into this world.

Mrs. Budd went on. "God showed us so much mercy and grace, and everywhere we look, we see His love. We have so much of it that we wanted to share it with someone else." She had been looking at me the whole time, but now her look seemed to bore right through my eyes, into my heart and my soul. "I believe that someone happens to be you. I don't know if you accept this or not, but I trust with all my heart that God chose you especially and brought us together for a reason, just like He chose to bless us with Matthew and Titus." She paused. "Do you think that there is a special reason God brought you here?"

I could feel a lump rising in my throat. I tried to push it down, to not let Mrs. Budd know that I was feeling any emotion toward her. It felt disloyal to think of the Budds as my family, when I was sure that at least part of my *real* family still existed. Yet in truth, her words touched me so much and the whole family was so kind and inviting that it was hard not to accept them. Something in me began to let loose. But then, suddenly, I felt myself snap back again. I had to stay strong! I couldn't doubt! What if my father could see me giving up hope of his ever coming back for me? What would he think? Would he be so disappointed in me that he wouldn't want me back again? Mrs. Budd's eyes were still looking into me, full of concern and care. I almost couldn't take it; I had to look away. I peeked at her out of the corner of my eye, and finally answered,

"Maybe I could believe it."

Mrs. Budd still kept eye contact with me. "If there is ever anything you want to talk about, I'm here for you."

I nodded and quickly turned away, knowing I couldn't bear to sit there much longer without crying. I climbed the stairs and went into my room. *My* room. It had such a neat feeling about it. I felt like that was one place where I really belonged. It was the one place I felt safe. Taking slow breaths to calm myself, I sat down on my bed. My fingers ran over the coverlet, tracing the patterns on the quilt. I looked around and breathed deeply. And I thought. I didn't even know what I was thinking about; I just thought.

I pushed myself off of my bed. The light in my room had changed. I blinked and realized that I must have fallen asleep. I smelled supper cooking in the kitchen. Slowly, yet still timidly, I walked down-stairs. The boys were watching a video in the living room. I glanced at the screen and I gathered that it was a cartoon about a builder whose building machines talked.

"There you are!" Mrs. Budd turned around and smiled at me. "You're just in time for supper." She stooped to check something in the oven, and then stood up again and set about chopping vegetables.

I stood there for a moment, and then for lack of anything better to do with my time, I picked out a cucumber and started chopping along with Mrs. Budd.

"Why, thank you, Saranna!" Mrs. Budd said, appreciatively.

Out of the corner of my eye I saw Mr. Budd working on the computer in a separate room off of the hallway. Presently, he stood up and walked into the kitchen.

"Looks like you two ladies have supper under control," he commented as he gave Mrs. Budd a kiss.

Mrs. Budd smiled back. "Yup, thanks to the help of Saranna." I felt my face grow red, even as I managed a small smile. I had only chopped a cucumber. Nevertheless, Mr. Budd smiled and gave me a pat on the back. It felt...*good* to be appreciated. Perhaps, there was a chance that I actually did matter to someone.

I set the salad bowl on the table as Mrs. Budd called into the living room for the boys to turn off the TV. We all sat down at the table, and Mr. Budd said a blessing like the night before.

"Grampy and Grammy are coming to see us tomorrow," Mrs. Budd announced as she filled plates. "My mom and dad live just five minutes away from here," she explained to me. "So does my sister, Aunt Jocelyn."

I nodded. I wondered if they would be kind like Mr. and Mrs. Budd. I couldn't say why, but I was almost scared to meet them. Maybe they would not like me. I didn't belong here, anyway.

Later that night back in my room, the words, "Heavenly Father" still echoed around in my head. I glanced over at the big book that was still sitting on my lamp stand. Did it tell about this Heavenly Father?

CHAPTER FOUR:

———————⋅⋅———————

The next day, as planned, Mrs. Budd's parents and sister came over. I hung back while Mr. Budd greeted them at the front door. Titus and Matthew ran out of the playroom like little rockets, racing to be the first to hug their grandparents.

"And this must be Saranna," the older lady exclaimed, coming toward me. I half hid myself behind Mrs. Budd. Mrs. Budd awkwardly walked forward with me lagging behind. I raised my eyes to look into the old lady's face. She had wrinkles around her cheeks, yet her eyes held a certain sparkle and her smile was the kind that instantly made me feel at ease. As she came closer to me, I slowly, still staring at her, stepped forward to meet her outstretched arms.

"I'm Grammy," she said, her smile growing bigger still. She patted the arm of her husband, who was standing behind her. "And this is Grampy."

The older man had thick glasses and equally as many wrinkles as his wife. He also had the same kind face. "Hello," he said, and he shook my hand. "Glad to meet you finally!"

"I'm Auntie Jocelyn," said a pretty young lady, who definitely looked related to Mrs. Budd. She was being pulled away by Matthew and Titus, however, and didn't have a chance to join the small crowd that was surrounding me. I was, in a sense, glad. I felt suffocated with everyone crowded around, staring at me.

Everyone was silent, and it felt like an awkward silence. They were just waiting for me to say something, but I didn't know what to say.

"I-I didn't know...I had a fan club here," I stuttered.

For some reason everyone started laughing. Mrs. Budd then invited everyone into the kitchen for some tea and coffee. She offered me a mug of peppermint tea. I took it. Everyone was sitting around the table, sipping their hot drinks and talking about boring things like gardens, gas prices, and tea flavors.

I stared into my mug. In one of my foster families, we used to have a daily tea time at 4 o'clock. The clock would chime and the lady of the house would beckon everyone into the stately dining room where her nice tea tray was sitting on the table. She would pour the tea ever so gracefully into the dainty tea cups. If someone spilled even one drop, she would nearly faint, and that unfortunate person would get sent to their room without supper.

The steam from the tea blanketed my face, making my eyes water and my neck feel moist.

The liquid in my mug began to grow blurry as I sat, reminiscing.

Suddenly I realized that everyone was staring at me. I looked up from my daydreaming and faced their eyes.

"I was just asking if you wanted to play with Auntie Jocelyn and the boys," Mrs. Budd said.

I nodded hurriedly as I pushed my chair away from the table, glad for a reason to get away from their chatter and stares. I started down the hallway, but instead of heading for the playroom, I veered off to the left of the hall, into the bathroom. I shut the door behind me and turned around to face the mirror above the sink. I looked at myself. The same dark brown, almost black hair, ocean-green eyes, pointy nose, and rounded face that I had sported my whole life reflected back at me. I didn't see what was so special about me that they would look so intently at.

I think Mrs. Budd sensed that I had become uncomfortable, so she politely dismissed her family after about half an hour. The boys responded by whining that they didn't get to play with Auntie Jocelyn long enough, but Mr. Budd told them that there would be a next time.

After dinner clean-up, I was just retreating upstairs when Mrs. Budd stopped me and said,

"Hey Saranna, could I hang out in your room for a bit with you?"

A surge of–*something*–hit me. It was a feeling I had never felt before. Half of me was excited at the prospect of having another female interested in 'hanging out' with me, and yet the other half felt some sort of disappointment or uncertainty that someone I barely knew was going to intrude into 'my' space. I shrugged.

"Yeah, I guess so."

So Mrs. Budd followed me up to my room. She closed the door and sat down on the bed next to me.

"How are you doing?" she started out with.

I shrugged at her again. It's my favorite way of communicating, mostly because I never know how to respond to personal questions.

"Okay, I guess."

Inside though, I was not okay. I felt like a ship tossed about on a stormy sea, not knowing which way to turn, with not even the light from a star to guide it or give the sailors a beam of hope. I felt shut out from this new world, locked inside myself. It was a familiar feeling, one that I had felt for most of my life. It was a strange kind of protection.

Mrs. Budd looked at me for a minute. Then she let her gaze wander about the room. I saw her eyes rest on my nightstand.

"Did you see this gift that we left for you?" she asked, reaching for the large book.

I nodded. "Hmm-hmm."

She held the book in her lap. "Do you know what it is?"

I shook my head ever so slightly.

"This is a Bible. It's a love letter from your King."

"A...*what*??" I stammered.

"A love letter from your King." She looked at me. "Do you know that you were created by God for a special purpose? He loves you. He sent His son, Jesus, to earth two thousand years ago to die in the most horrible way so that we could become His children. Here, let me show you," she said as she picked up the book and flipped some pages. "1 John 3:1 says, 'See what kind of love the Father has given to us, that we should be called children of God...' Because we have all disobeyed God, we didn't deserve that love, but He gave it to us anyway."

I thought about what she was saying. I guess that was why Mr. Budd had prayed, "Heavenly Father." I still didn't get it, though...yet I couldn't explain what I didn't understand about it. The explanation seemed incomplete, but I couldn't put my finger on it.

Mrs. Budd must have figured that I had had enough, because she gently closed the Bible and set it back down on the bed. She got up to leave, but hesitated at the door. She turned back around and said, "Saranna, God is a King; the King of Kings, the Bible says. That means that if you accept His invitation to become His child, you will be a Princess."

And then she left.

Days fell into a sort of lazy routine. I was slowly getting adjusted to my new lifestyle, but I still didn't feel the peace that everyone thinks someone is supposed to feel after getting "rescued" from a hopeless situation and adopted into a loving family. I didn't know what was wrong with me.

The first Sunday passed just like another Saturday. Mr. Budd stayed home from work and everyone took it easy. We had a short "Bible Study," but that was all. The second week, however, Mr. Budd announced that we would be going to church.

France is known for its beautiful churches, so of course I had some exposure to them. In other words, I wasn't shocked or offended by the word "church," like some people I've known. I'd never really tried to understand what religion was all about, though. I had figured I'd worry about it later.

The churches that I had been to in France were quite dull—long sermons with the congregation following specific regulations and reciting prayers at specific times. I could only assume that the churches in America would be similar.

But when I walked through the plain-looking white doors of the building, as the sounds of piano, guitar, and singing floated out, I began to wonder: had I been correct in my presumptions?

CHAPTER FIVE

W e entered the sanctuary and sat down. I must have been staring around bug-eyed, because Matthew and Titus were looking at me like I was sick or something.

Up at the front there was a simple stage with one step leading up to it. To the left, in the back corner, stood three singers behind microphones, and a young lady playing the piano. Toward the right corner was a man strumming on a guitar. At the front of the stage there was a pulpit with a wooden cross nailed to the front of it. On the left and right sides of the back wall were paintings: one of a shepherd holding a staff in his hand and guiding a sheep between two cliff walls, and one of a dove ascending into a clouded sky.

A man in a coat and tie would step up to the pulpit at the end of every song and announce the next song's title. He would then either invite the people to stand up, or direct them to sit down. My legs started getting tired of all the up and down. Finally, after what seemed like a bazillion songs, the singers and musicians stepped down from the stage and took their seats among the congregation. The man who had been announcing the songs stood up again and walked behind the pulpit.

"Good morning," he began, and all the people then called back "Good morning!"

"Yes, it is a wonderful morning to be gathered together to worship the Lord. We have special reason to rejoice today. The Budd family is finally celebrating the arrival of their adopted daughter, who is with us today—"

At this, everyone began clapping and turning to where we sat to smile at me. Were I measuring my level of self consciousness at this point, I probably would have broken the meter. I couldn't bear to picture how red my face must have been turning.

The pastor then went on with his message, and I struggled to listen and stay interested. To be perfectly honest, he talked so much like Mrs. Budd did sometimes that I could barely understand him. He kept saying things like, "the Kingdom of God" and man's "sin-nature." What was I supposed to do with all this?

After 20 minutes, I struggled to hold back a yawn. I knew that he would probably be going strong for at least another half-hour, and I found myself counting minutes on the clock about every 30 seconds.

I looked around the room. I didn't see many other children, only a few teenagers, two babies, and a brother and sister that looked to be about five or six. *"Go figure there aren't more kids,"* I thought.

My attention was snapped back as I sensed the pastor concluding the sermon. I felt guilty for spacing out and tried to listen as attentively as I could muster for the last few minutes. I hoped that could make up for my lack of attention in the beginning.

The pastor gave the benediction and everyone began to stand up and mill about the sanctuary. I didn't know whether to stand or sit, so I ended up sort of in between the two positions, looking at Mr. and Mrs. Budd to see what they would do. Mr. Budd stood up and Mrs. Budd stayed sitting down. Great. Now I was really stuck, and my legs were getting sore from my half-standing half-sitting. Finally I decided to stand up, and hoped that that would make me blend into the crowd more.

Yeah, right. EVERYONE wanted to talk with us! I was uncomfortable being the center of attention. I couldn't even count how many people said, "Oh, I'm so glad you're here finally!" I think equally as many people said, "We're so happy for you!"

I wanted to tell them that they had no idea. It was just sickening how wrong they got everything. I wanted to vomit and hide in the bathroom. We began to make our way into the lobby, but it took us at least 20 minutes what with the constant crowd around us! I tried to shelter myself behind Mr. Budd. He was big and tall, perfect for hiding behind. But people are funny; if you try to avoid them, it sometimes seems as if that gives them more incentive to find you.

Once we finally got to the lobby and the crowd began to thin out a little, (I think it was the smell of the fresh-brewed coffee that got them), I motioned for Mr. Budd to lean over so that I could talk to him. Even then, I had to stand on tiptoes to whisper in his ear, "Are people always like this here?" Mr. Budd smiled and chuckled in his soft way...just before he was greeted by another couple.

After the insanity of church, it seemed so good to be able to relax on my bed, all by myself. That is, until Mrs. Budd knocked on the door.

"What are you doing in here?" she asked, after I told her to come in.

I shrugged. "Nothing, really."

She nodded. "So what did you think of church?"

Well, she had asked the 10 million dollar question. I wanted to respond, 'What do I think of church? I think that it is filled with freaky, misunderstanding people.' I knew that would be extremely disrespectful to say out loud, though, so instead I replied, "Is everyone always that crazy and loud?"

Mrs. Budd tried not to laugh, but she couldn't keep a smile from lighting up her face, like her smiles always did. "No, it's not always that way. They were just all so excited to invite you into their lives. You see, a church is not just a group of people who come together every week to listen to an hour long sermon. It is supposed to be a family."

"What do you mean, 'a family'?" I asked.

"Remember how I read you that verse from 1 John that said God adopted us into His family?"

I nodded.

"Well, a church is a group of people who have all been adopted by the Lord because they have received Him as their Savior. When a bunch of people are adopted by one person, they become brothers and sisters, right? It's no different with God. When you accept Him as your heavenly father and ask Him to forgive your sins—all the ways we have broken God's law—you are welcomed into His big family."

All this Mrs. Budd had explained slowly and patiently. I could actually follow her reasoning. But I still had a question on where I stood.

"So, if someone doesn't 'accept Him,' as you say, are they still a part of that big family?"

"This book," Mrs. Budd said hesitantly, motioning to the Bible on the side of my bed, "can explain that answer much better than I can. Basically, Jesus' free gift of salvation is open to anyone who is willing to repent and believe. When they do that, they become a part of His family and are given an inheritance in Heaven. God doesn't force His gift on us, so He won't give it to you unless you decide that you really want it. But you have to make that choice for yourself. No matter what you decide, the church, or the Body of Christ, will still be there to support you, but you won't be 'related' as the people who have accepted Jesus are. Does that make sense?"

I stared into space, debriefing what she had just said. I felt like she was still talking in code language, because I didn't understand what all of the Christian lingo meant, exactly, but I thought I could understand what she was saying. Finally, I felt ready to reply.

"I think so."

Mrs. Budd nodded. "Good." She paused for a few seconds. "I just came up to see how you were doing."

"Okay." My answer was short and sweet...and deceitful.

Mrs. Budd nodded again, but her eyes still bore into me. She seemed to read my soul. I sensed that no matter how hard I concealed it, she would still know the truth about me.

"Are you sure?"

Okay, now things were getting a bit more complicated. I had two choices: admit my feelings, or lie again. I didn't want to admit my feelings. Not to her.

"Sort of." It was in the middle of my two choices, and I hoped that she got the hint not to question any further.

"Okay. I'm here if you change your mind, though." She gave me a hug then walked out of the room.

CHAPTER SIX

After three weeks, I started to get into the routine of life with the Budds. Mrs. Budd did homeschool lessons with us every day. She got me my own math curriculum, and I practiced multiplication and division. I read one chapter of a book every day then answered questions about it for literature. I studied a science textbook and did English lessons in a workbook. The English work was the most difficult, but overall, the things that I was learning in the Budd household were really neat. For the first time in my life, I actually enjoyed learning and looked forward to my school work each day.

My arrival generated less attraction now, (to my relief!) although we still received an occasional card saying congratulations to me. Church was less of an epic each week, although people still seemed to regard me as "special" or "amazing." It was NOT true. I was so below-average. My pain seemed so great that sometimes I only felt half-human. No one here appeared to understand.

Nevertheless, life was settling down. Until one day, that all changed.

Co-op registration was coming up. Mrs. Budd approached me one day and asked me which classes I wanted to take. She gave me a list of all the classes offered and pointed out the ones that were my grade level. She told me that if nothing looked attractive for a certain period, I could do study hall. I thought *that* sounded attractive, just because it was solitary, but to appease her I did check out some of the classes. After one quick look, I immediately eliminated about 3 choices. I looked again. The Earth Science class sounded interesting, because I had really been enjoying my science studies lately. Another class that grabbed my attention was an art class. It sounded fun to be able to paint and learn about different colors and techniques. Art was in second period. The science class was in first period. I couldn't see anything else I liked, so I asked Mrs. Budd if I could take study hall for third period.

"That would be fine," she responded. "Did you find any other classes interesting?"

I showed her my two picks. She tried to point out some other classes that she thought might be fun for me to take, but I stayed with my original choices. So Mrs. Budd consented, and she showed me how to use a special sheet of printed paper to write out my choices for each hour. She told me that I had to pick second choices as well, just in case there were too many other students in my first choices. I did, but I hoped that I would get into all of my first choices...*sincerely* hoped.

Registration night took place in mid-July. Mrs. Budd went alone to register all of us. Titus, Matthew, and I waited in anxious anticipation. We were all hoping that we would get into our first choices. Matthew and Titus' classes had been the subject of dinner conversations for weeks preceding registration night. I could tell they were excited and that this meant a lot to them. I wondered if by the end of the year it would mean a lot to me, too.

Mr. Budd had made a special exception for the boys' bedtime so that they could be awake when Mrs. Budd came home to tell them which classes they had gotten into.

Three hours later, a tired Mrs. Budd walked through the front door. The boys rushed up to her and nearly tackled her with their hugs and questions. I had a bit more self control, but I knew that if my own father or mother had just walked in the door instead of Mrs. Budd, I would be acting just like little 4 and 5 year old boys.

"What classes did we get?" the boys cried, jumping up and down.

"Whoa, slow down!" Mrs. Budd reprimanded as she leaned over to kiss Mr. Budd.

The boys "ushered" her to the sofa—well, more like dragged her! — still pleading for the news.

"Alright, alright," she laughed. "Titus, you are going to your preschool class, Matthew, you got into Character First, the reading class with Mrs.

Brown, and Gym class. Saranna, you got all your first choices."

The boys whooped and hurrahed and I let out a sigh that I didn't realize I had been holding in. I figured that since the boys were being so loud, no one would notice it if I threw a whoop in there, too.

Even after we all stopped yelling, the boys were still hyper and were bouncing all over the place.

"When do we start?" I asked, trying to use as calm and neutral a voice as I could.

"In one month," Mrs. Budd answered. "We'll have to be able to get out the door by 8:45 in the morning every Friday," she added pointedly at Titus and Matthew. It sounded like a warning, I guessed because they were always waking up around 8:30. From habit, I just woke up between 6 and 6:30. I could get my schoolwork done in my room while enjoying a couple hours of peace.

At any rate, with two little boys, it always took forever to get ready to go somewhere. I'm a teenage girl, and it only takes me half as long to get ready as the boys and Mrs. Budd. I usually have a book ready so that I have something to do while I'm waiting for them. I knew that if we were to be going to this Friday morning co-op, we would all have to start practicing now.

Mr. Budd was finally able to get the boys settled down enough to be herded upstairs, but even after I had gone to bed, I could still hear bumps and thumps and giggling coming from their bedroom.

Those weeks of "practice" went by so slowly. I don't get the concept of time. It speeds up whenever you are late and it slows down whenever you are waiting for something to happen. Mrs. Budd took me shopping a few nights after Registration night for a backpack. It was just her and me, and I rode in the front seat with her. It was so quiet and peaceful. I could tell it was a good break for her, too. And of course, she took the opportunity to ask me how I was doing. I was getting pretty good at my usual answer. She also asked me if I was excited for co-op. I shrugged. I said I wasn't sure what there was to be excited about. She just smiled.

At the store, we took our cart to the "School Supplies" section. There were so many options for a backpack! Mrs. Budd and I spent at least 20 minutes comparing colors, trying them on, debating the craziest designs, then the plainest, before we finally agreed on the best one for me. I loved it! It had gray trim, and raspberry, violet, and indigo paint streaks danced across the white background. It even came with a silver flower charm.

I don't know how to describe our night. It was... special, amazing, nice...and even more than that. I felt like I was someone special; for the first time in my life someone was truly interested in me and invested their time to buy me something I really liked. It puzzled me.

The day after our shopping trip, I packed all the supplies I would need in my backpack: science textbook, art smock, pencils, colored pencils, pen, eraser, sketch pad, and a list of extra work that I could do in study hall.

One month is a long time, and the days seemed to creep by at a snail's pace. The extra time was probably good for Mrs. Budd to get prepared, but all it did for me was give me more time to freak out. During that month, I checked my backpack to make sure that I had everything in there so many times; I suspect I did it in my sleep. I had memorized not only all the supplies and in which pocket they were kept, but also every nook, every cranny, every seam, and every hanging thread on the backpack itself. Just looking at the backpack gave me such a sense of beauty. Such a warm feeling of...love, maybe, washed over me whenever I gazed on it. I hung it over the back of the chair at my desk so that I could see it from my bed while I was falling asleep. I laid out my favorite shirt to wear with my best pair of jeans weeks in advance, just in case for some reason they didn't make it through the wash in time. I dreamed countless times about the first day of co-op. So many, in fact, that sometimes I would wonder if I was just re-living what had already happened.

Finally, it was only one more week before the first day. I did all my chores and schoolwork as if in a trance and my backpack checks went from maybe one or two a day to about nine or ten a day. I got so tired of unzipping and zipping again. I was annoyed at myself for constantly checking something that I already knew about as well as I knew myself, but I couldn't help it!

On Tuesday of that week, Mr. Budd announced that he had to make a quick trip to the hardware store to pick up some supplies for work. "Saranna, would you come with me?" he asked.

What could I say? "No"? So two minutes later, I was reluctantly buckling myself into his pickup truck, and riding down the short route to the hardware store.

Mr. Budd's work truck was messy. Old paper cups and little pieces of paper and plastic wrappers filled the console between him and me. It looked like the floor of the cockpit hadn't been vacuumed in a year. Wood splinters and sand covered it, and mud stains popped up here and there. Otherwise, the truck had a nice pine smell, and Mr. Budd was good company...even though we didn't utter a word to each other the whole 10 minute drive.

Once we got to the store, Mr. Budd motioned for me to follow him into the building. We went to the front desk and Mr. Budd talked with the man there for about three minutes. The man then led us to the back of the store. Mr. Budd was picking up an order of specially cut boards for his boss, and he had to carry them all the way from the storeroom in back to his truck out front.

"Saranna, can you help me with these?" he asked, motioning to the other end of a stack of boards that he was tying together. So I helped him carry them through the store, across the windy parking lot, and load them into the pickup. It felt good to work with my hands and use my muscles again. The wind blew my hair into my face and whipped at my shirt, but I didn't care. A few more trips and a handshake later, we were on our way home again.

Back on the road, Mr. Budd broke our silence. "I have something to give to you, Saranna," he said. I looked over at him as he reached into his pocket and pulled out what looked like an IPod.

"It's for study hall," he said as he handed it to me. "I thought that you would like some music to listen to during that hour."

I couldn't believe my eyes. I couldn't trust my ears. But it was true! I had seen rich, popular kids at school in France listening to music on their IPods, and I had always been envious. It seemed that having an IPod got you the label "cool" and put you in the "in" crowd. I never in a million years thought that I would ever own one, though! Who would've guessed that me, a little, insignificant orphan from France, would actually own an IPod!

I wanted to hug Mr. Budd right then and there, but I had to wait until he stopped the car in our driveway. Then I leaned over the messy console and hugged him as hard as I could.

"Thank you!" I whispered with tears in my eyes. Mr. Budd kissed me on the head and hugged me back. For some reason, it didn't feel weird at all.

CHAPTER SEVEN

———◦———

Darkness pressed against my eyelids, but light was piercing through, trying to get in. My alarm was going off, and I was rolling over, groping, reaching...there! It was off. I forced my eyes opened and looked at the green, square, lit up numbers: 6:18 am. Suddenly I sat up, my heart beating fast and my stomach fluttering excitedly. My brain tried to catch up with the rest of my body. Yes! Today was the day! Today was Friday. Friday the third of September. It was the first day of co-op!

Still feeling a bit sick from the butterflies trying to escape from my stomach, I literally jumped out of bed and tip-toed to the closet. As I tried to walk quietly, my whole body was shaking. My mind was racing. *"Wait, why am I trying to be quiet this morning?? Everyone else has to get up, too!"* I grabbed my clothes and crossed the hall to the bathroom.

I shivered. It had gotten colder over the night. Hurriedly, I slipped soap into my hands and scrubbed my face, then rinsed with warm water.

I dried myself on a towel, brushed my teeth and combed my hair. After tugging on my jeans and slipping my shirt over my head, I opened the drawer under the sink and rummaged in it until I found a hair elastic. I used the brush to fix my part and comb my hair smooth at the top while I gathered it up into a ponytail in the middle of my head. When I was finished, I tried to take a deep breath, but it ended up being shallow and shaky. I looked closely at my face in the mirror. Yes, my hair looked alright. I took a little water and wet the tiny hairs that stuck up near my part. Now it was perfect. I stepped back and studied the full effect. My light pink shirt accented with the silver-sparkly flower designs looked great with my dark hair. I had taken the charm that came with my backpack and strung it onto a piece of delicate chain that was left over in Mrs. Budd's craft supplies. The necklace was now clasped around my neck. My usual pair of jeans looked extraordinary today. I had chosen my newest pair of white heel socks to wear under my sneakers. Yes, I looked cleaner, fresher, and prettier than I think I ever had in my life.

Just one thought of all those other kids who would be at co-op today, though, made me want to curl up in my bed all day and forget the whole thing. Would they be mean to me? Would they think that I was not good enough for them? Would they know my past and look down on me because of it? Would the parents crowd around me and treat me like the people at church had?

I was nervous and self conscious all over again. I would never fit in! Why was I even here? Why was I so different from everyone else? Why couldn't my father have come back for me? Our lives could have been so much happier together! As I pondered these frustrating thoughts, I stared at myself in the mirror and realized that a tear was trickling down my cheek. But I couldn't cry! My only chance to fit in with all those other kids was to look my prettiest today, so I couldn't afford to let my eyes turn red and my face to look all funny for the rest of the day.

Before I let my brain dwell on these things a moment longer, I opened the bathroom door and rushed out into the hallway. I gingerly took my backpack off the chair that it had been waiting on all month, then picked my IPod up from its special place of honor on my desk, and slipped it into the outside pocket of my backpack. There wasn't as much chance of it getting squashed by my science textbook there. I smiled to myself. Mr. Budd didn't know that the IPod might just give me the boost of self-confidence I needed today to carry me through. Maybe, *just* maybe, he cared about me like my real father. What if he did? Suddenly my smile disappeared. If I had two fathers, and they both cared about me like a real daddy, would I have to pick who I was to be loyal to? Then there was this "Heavenly Father" that I kept hearing about thrown into the mix...what was I supposed to do with *three* fathers?? I shook my head. I would have to think about it later.

One glance at my alarm clock told me it was time to scram. It was nearly 7:00.

I took a quick peek into the boys' room on my way downstairs. They were still breathing evenly in sleep, although as I was leaving Matthew stirred a bit. I walked down the stairs, running my hand down the smooth railing thoughtfully. It felt cool to my fingers. My socks made my feet slip down the stairs as easily as a knife slips through butter. The edge of each stair pressing against the sole of my foot felt good to me. There was no better time for peaceful thought than in the morning. Most of all the feel-good moments in my life had happened in the early morning hours. Late afternoon, though...a storm cloud blew over my countenance. That was when they had taken him. I hated late afternoon.

I entered the kitchen to find Mrs. Budd already bustling around. Even though I was sure she was stressed, she appeared as her normal, cheery self, interrupting her work to give me a lovely "Good morning!" greeting. She turned around and looked me up and down.

"You look gorgeous today, Saranna!"

Even though I felt a warm blush cover my face, Mrs. Budd had given me another vote of confidence that brought my levels almost up to normal. I got out a bowl and a spoon, and began fixing myself a dish of cereal. When I first started living with the Budds, Mrs. Budd asked me what I liked to eat, and she tried to cook meals that I was used to. However, I had gradually become more open to trying different flavors and menus. Just recently I had started trying cereal and fruit instead of my usual toast, jam, and yogurt.

"The boys aren't up yet," I informed Mrs. Budd, as I sat down at the table to eat.

"Yeah, I know." She responded with a reassuring smile to me. "I'll go wake them in about five minutes." Then, with a twinkle in her eye, "If they wake up before then, we'll know!"

I laughed a little. I knew what she meant. When the boys got up, the word "quiet" wasn't in their vocabulary. A certain measure of bumps and thumps coming from the ceiling was all the affirmation anyone would need!

By seven-thirty, the whole Budd family was awake and bustling. Mr. Budd's heavy footsteps echoed down the hall as he walked back and forth from his office, getting ready to go to work. The boys scampered here and there with their light, quick, pitter-pattering footsteps, and Mrs. Budd's soft, even footsteps were walking about the kitchen cleaning up from breakfast and packing lunches and snacks. Apparently, after co-op was finished, we were going to the park to visit with a few other families.

As for me, I was taking my time, and in my usual, steady pace, loading all of our things into the van for Mrs. Budd: backpacks and coolers, purses and water bottles. The amount of things we were taking was unbelievable. Despite all that, we did end up getting everyone in the van at 8:30 and were almost ready to take off...but then Mrs. Budd remembered that she had left the address for the park somewhere in the house. Ten minutes later, we were finally on our way—for real this time.

The 20 minute ride to co-op was pretty quiet. The boys were still sleepy, so the only sound that came from them was an occasional yawn. Mrs. Budd was silent as well. I suspect that she was still tired, too. Of course, I didn't say anything. The classical music playing softly from the radio filled the silence. I don't know what it is about being in a group of tired people, but it makes me somewhat sleepy, too.

Mrs. Budd pulled into the parking lot of a huge church building. There were many other cars in the parking lot, and people were walking to and from the doors of the building. Mrs. Budd found a parking space and then we unloaded all the boys, and backpacks, and purses, and lunch sacks, and water bottles. Mrs. Budd was meticulous about making sure that each snack sack and water bottle made it into the boys' backpacks, and took a whole two minutes explaining to them that they had to keep all of their stuff together. I sighed and quietly slipped my snack and water into my backpack. This whole thing with little boys was such a procedure!

By the time we finally made it into the building, the boys had enough pent-up excitement to launch a rocket halfway to Mars. The lobby was filled with people. Mrs. Budd held onto our hands and we made our way to a folding table in the back of the room. There sat three file boxes, each filled with folders that had last names written on them. Mrs. Budd found the box marked "A-G", searched for the folder marked "Budd", then opened it and took out a bunch of nametags. She handed one to each of us. Titus got a sticker with his name on it, but the rest of us got a plastic pouch hung on a cord. I looked at the green paper in mine. It said:

Saranna
Budd

Suddenly, I felt my cheeks grow hot and my spine started prickling. I had never seen that name before. My name had always been Saranna Moreau—Saranna M. at my orphanage. An overwhelming sense of change washed over me as I reflected for the first time that adoption was completely switching my identity. I looked down at the bold, black letters again. I did not know who Saranna Budd was. How was I supposed to be her if I didn't even know who she was?

I didn't feel Mrs. Budd guide me into the big gymnasium. The next thing I knew, a hush fell over the crowd that had assembled around a PA system in the back of the gym. I moved around a bit until I could see through the crowd enough to catch a glimpse of a woman speaking into the microphone. She introduced herself as Andrea Siller, and then she focused everyone's attention to the projection mounted on the wall behind her. I realized that it was the words to a song. In one voice, all the many people in the gym began singing the words together:

"Then sings my soul, my Savior God, to thee.

How great Thou art.

How great Thou art.

Then sings my soul, my Savior God, to thee.

How great Thou art.

How great Thou art."

I didn't even join in the singing. I couldn't follow along with the words because they made no sense to me. As everyone else bowed their head in prayer, I glanced down at my shoes but kept my eyes open, staring at all the other legs and shoes around me. Before I knew it, the crowd began to stir as Mrs. Siller dismissed the infants and preschoolers first. Mrs. Budd turned to me, and I recognized a worried look behind her eyes.

"I have to take Titus to his class. Will you know where to go?"

I opened my mouth to answer, but I couldn't make a sound. My throat felt tight and dry. The honest answer was no. And now, I wasn't even sure I cared.

"That's okay; you can follow Matthew. Matthew, if Saranna shows you the room number, will you lead her there before your class?"

"Sure, Mom!" replied Matthew, clearly proud of himself for getting the job of being responsible for me. Mrs. Budd was being pulled away toward the door by Titus, and over the noise of everyone else exiting the gym in different directions, I couldn't hear another word she said. But her ability to read my mind was sure getting annoying.

Matthew smiled up at me, holding my hand and swinging it between us.

"Don't worry, I'll show you where to go! Just follow me!" With that he grabbed my nametag, took a quick glance at the back, then dashed off down the hallway, dodging kids and adults of all ages and dragging me along behind.

Eventually, we arrived in front of a classroom that had the same number next to the door as the one on my nametag. He was out of breath from running and my cheeks were turning red from having everyone see a six year old leading me to my class. On the inside though, I was glad that he was there to help me. The more I thought about it, the more I realized that it would have been more embarrassing if I showed up to class late.

"Here's your first class. If you want, I can meet you here before snack and take you there, too." He beamed at me.

I struggled internally for a second or two, but then I smiled back at him. Just because I was battling complicated and hurtful feelings didn't mean I had to take it out on him.

"Thanks, Matthew! I don't know what I'd do without you," I said, trying to keep from sounding sarcastic.

Matthew, still beaming, shouted goodbye for the whole building to hear, then ran off so fast he nearly collided into an older man, and then almost fell down in his desperate effort to stop his momentum and dodge around him. Quickly, I turned and walked into the classroom. It was a simple carpeted room with a whiteboard on one wall, three long tables with chairs set up to make three sides of a square, and a window at the far end of the room. Four boys and two other girls were already there, seated at the table facing the whiteboard. The class was filling up quickly, so I claimed a seat down at the very end of the tables, away from everyone else. I set my backpack down gently on the floor at my feet, and leaned my elbows on the table, trying to look as calm, cool, and collected as I could—trying to fake that I belonged there.

I watched other students trickle into the room. Most came in groups of two or three. Many were loud and talkative. Soon, a group of four girls walked in, chatting loudly and laughing. One girl seemed to catch my eye. She had been at the center of the group, but when she saw me, she left her friends who were finding chairs at the other end of the table and came toward me.

"Hi!" she said cheerfully. She was a brown haired girl with a dark complexion and wide, brown eyes that sparkled as if they were Christmas lights. Her lips were parted in a friendly smile that showed her green braces, and her voice sounded airy and excited.

"My name's Grace," she said. "Are you new?"

I was still trying to recover from the shock of her taking an interest in me, and I sat with my mouth open for what seemed like forever until I could get my voice to do what I wanted it to do.

"Yeah," I whispered, hoping she would get the point and not make a big show of it. "I'm Saranna."

"Good to meet you! It's kinda crazy in here, huh?"

I almost laughed out loud. *That* coming from *her*? Less than a minute ago she had been laughing and talking just as loud as everyone else! She obviously wasn't bothered by it.

"Yeah," I said, trying to stifle a snort.

"That's 'cause we're all so excited." Grace said matter-of-factly. "Are you excited?"

That question shouldn't have caught me off guard because I knew the answer to it, but I guess I wasn't used to admitting how I felt to strangers.

"Um...ah—well, I...I guess...I don't know." I stammered.

Grace nodded, seemingly satisfied with my answer. "You'll probably get used to it quickly. And by then everyone will be settled down a bit, too."

She probably would have said more, but just then a grown woman who was obviously the teacher walked into the room and took her place in front of the whiteboard. Introductions were made and soon we were all busy diving into the first lesson.

CHAPTER EIGHT

True to his word, as soon as class was dismissed, before I even had a chance to figure out which hall to look down first, Matthew was there, standing in front of me with that big smile of his.

"Come on! This way is snack."

So again I was dragged down the halls by a six year old, trying my best to not run into anyone or through any big clusters of kids who were walking together.

"Everyone's always together. Because they belong," I thought sadly.

Matthew and I entered the snack room, which was a large hall with a tall ceiling. Sunlight poured in from the windows and lit on groups of kids, young and old, eating snacks. The sounds of talking and laughing echoed off the walls and made it hard to hear anything else.

Matthew walked over to a group of younger kids who were all sitting in a circle on the tiled floor. He looked back to see if I was coming, too.

I hesitated. Did I really want to be associated with all those little kids? Maybe I should just find a place and sit down alone. But as I looked around, I realized that there weren't many places that could be classified as "alone." Finally, I gave into Matthew and uneasily joined his group.

Matthew got out his snack and nodded for me to do the same. I reached into my backpack and drew out the brown paper bag. I tried to eat a few of the curly chips, but I found that I wasn't hungry. There were some new tastes that I just couldn't get used to, yet. Simply a plain piece of bread would have been more to my liking. I looked around the hall. There were so many people! My eyes lit on a few that I recognized from my first class. My gaze was suddenly drawn to the girl who had sat next to me, Grace. At about the same time, Grace saw me. I quickly looked away so that she wouldn't think I was staring, but she waved to me and beckoned for me to come over to her.

I looked at Matthew. He was so busy stuffing his mouth full and laughing with his friends that surely he wouldn't notice if I left. I looked back to Grace and then made my decision. I stood up and slowly made my way across the hall, picking my way through huddles of people.

Grace smiled at me as I sat down next to her. "Saranna, this is my friend, Karolyn." She motioned to a girl about my age with curly red hair and a round face. "Karolyn, this is my new friend, Saranna," Grace finished the introduction.

"Hi," said Karolyn, not gruffly but not exactly warm and inviting, either.

"Hi," I whispered back to her.

Silence fell. Karolyn and Grace were chewing and I was feeling uneasy, glancing around the room, trying to find a way of escape.

The snack time lasted only 5 minutes, but it was the longest 5 minutes of my life. When a grownup lady shouted above all the other voices that snack time was over and it was time to go to our next class, I gladly scooped up my backpack and dashed down the hall.

My quick getaway was halted when I suddenly realized that I didn't know where to go. *"Oh, well,"* I thought. *"I can figure it out on my own. After all, I'm not a baby!"*

I moved over to the side of the hallway to make way for the huge rush of kids that came pouring out of the snack room. I glanced at the back of my nametag and found that the room number for my next class was 128. I looked at the doorway nearest to me and found the numbers 116. I started walking to my left and discovered that the next room number was 114. I was confused. *Did I miss a room?* One quick glance back down the hall told me no, I had not skipped a room. *"They must be counting the rooms by twos,"* I thought. *"Of all the things! How confusing."*

After a couple more minutes of searching, I arrived at the door of a classroom that had the same number as my nametag: 128. The class was just about to begin, so I ducked in and settled in my seat quickly, all the while trying not to let my face turn as red as beets.

"Welcome to art class, everyone!" the teacher began warmly. "I'm Mrs. Greenholt. Let's go around the room and introduce ourselves, as I see there are some new people here." She smiled at me, and I sank lower down in my chair.

The girl sitting at the farthest right end of the table went first. Around the room we went, each girl or boy saying their first and last name. When my turn came, I said, "I'm Saranna." That was it.

Once introductions were finished, Mrs. Greenholt began a description of the course. "We're going to be studying different forms of art, including painting, sculpting, sketching, coloring, mosaics, and decoupage. Along the way, we'll also study famous artists from long ago."

Despite the awkward first impression, I predicted that I was going to like this class. Mrs. Greenholt had her assistant teachers pass out our own color wheels. I studied mine. It was two round pieces of paper clipped together, and when you twirled the top piece, you could see the different shades of a color you could make, just by adding another color. Mrs. Greenholt used the whiteboard to help explain primary colors and secondary colors. She also explained how colors such as red, orange, and yellow were called "warm" colors and shades of blue and green were called "cool" colors.

The hour was up all too quickly. I was sad to leave so soon.

Now I was on to Study Hall. I figured it didn't matter if I showed up late this hour, so I didn't stress out as I wandered down the halls, navigating my way to the Library.

As I pushed the door open, I saw that some other kids had already beaten me there. Three girls sat in a cluster at the far end of the Library, and one boy sat by himself at the other end of the room. A grown lady who was monitoring the study session was sitting off to one side reading a book.

I entered quietly, so as not to disturb anyone. The lady looked up from her reading and smiled sweetly at me.

"You must be Saranna," she said quietly. "Feel free to take a seat anywhere."

"Thank you," I returned in a whisper. I looked around the room and sat down in a chair right in the middle of the boy and the group of girls. I opened my backpack and took out some English homework that I was still working on from the past week. I spread it out on the table, and then inwardly smiled to myself. There was one other thing that I still had to take out. I gingerly reached down and unzipped the special pocket on the outside of my backpack. I reached in and drew out my IPod.

Mr. Budd had put soft, soothing songs on my IPod. I didn't recognize many of them, although they were all "Gospel songs," (or whatever they're called). All throughout my Study Hall period, I enjoyed listening to my music while struggling through my homework. English is much more complicated than French, in my mind. There are so many rules to keep straight, and some of the words don't even follow the rules, anyways! At least I didn't need to learn how to speak English. I already knew how because we spoke both French and English at the group home.

Once the hour was up, I could see people walking down the hallways through a little window in the Library door. The noise level began to grow in the classrooms next to us. After a few minutes, the lady who was monitoring Study Hall dismissed us and we began to pack up our things. I took my earbuds out and gently wrapped the chords around the IPod. After I safely stowed it away in its special pocket, I picked up my textbook and notebook and stashed them away in my backpack. I stood up and slung it over my shoulder and prepared myself to enter those now bustling halls.

It was like stepping out of a silent picture from a storybook and entering a natural disaster area. The difference between the halls and the quiet, serene room that I just left was so shocking to me that I stood rooted to the spot for what seemed like half a minute. I willed my feet to move so that I didn't look like a moron standing there staring with my mouth gaping open.

I slowly made my way to the lobby where Mrs. Budd had instructed us all to meet at the end of co-op. I had to wait around a bit, but I eventually found her with Matthew and Titus amidst the SEA of people, milling about and all talking at once.

Despite all that was going on around us, Mrs. Budd gave me one of her special smiles as I walked over to her—the one that said she was so glad to see me, even if I was a mess.

"Hi, Saranna! How did you fare?"

Thankfully, I'm good at taking the attention off of myself. "Well, Matthew got me to class safely." I couldn't help smiling at his sheepish grin.

Mrs. Budd's expression seemed to show that she already guessed half the events that had transpired during the past three hours, but I didn't let that bother me. Instead I helped to gather up all our stuff and load the whole crew back into the car once more.

I set my things on the floor of the passenger seat, then climbed in and shut the door behind me. Mrs. Budd kept getting stopped by other ladies who wanted to greet her or chat with her. I didn't know how anyone could stand all that stimulation!

CHAPTER NINE

Finally, Mrs. Budd loaded herself into the driver's seat and began arranging her things.

"Saranna, could you dig in my purse and find the address that I wrote down on a piece of notebook paper?" she asked me.

I unzipped the bag and rummaged around until I found the one she was looking for.

"Thanks!" she said appreciatively as I handed the sheet to her.

"So...how many people are going to be at the park?" I asked casually.

"We'll be meeting some families from co-op there, but I imagine it won't be too crowded. I think I've been to this park before, and it's really nice," Mrs. Budd replied.

I nodded absent mindedly. As we pulled out of the parking lot, I put my chin in my hand and leaned my forehead against the window. For some reason, the cool glass helped to cool me down. I hoped this afternoon would be a tiny bit more peaceful than this morning.

Since I was more awake now than I was driving to co-op, I was able to look around at the scenery as we drove. There were many houses, and an occasional field overgrown with tall, yellow grass. Stone walls popped up now and then, and the beautiful, striking colors of the trees captivated me. I had never seen anything quite like it. Each house that we passed had a characteristic of its own. Some were stately and modern, with big, elaborate doorways and windows, tall roofs and groomed lawns and gardens. Other places spoke as more of a home than a house, with varying heights, colors, and styles. The colorful shutters, distinguishable window shapes, and unique decorations in the yards all spoke for the different personalities of each owner. Sometimes we would pass a property with fenced in fields of horses or cows. I thought it was funny when I saw one of those big, modern houses right next to a short, shabby one that sat on a well-used, yet well-maintained property. I appreciated both styles, though each in different ways.

"How did you like co-op?" Mrs. Budd's voice called me out of my own head and brought me back to real life.

"The classes were nice," I offered.

Mrs. Budd nodded. "That's good."

I felt a bit uneasy, not knowing what else to say. Mrs. Budd continued the conversation with another question.

"What did you learn that was interesting to you?"

I figured it wasn't the right scenario to tell her about my "enlightenment" to English versus French, but I *had* enjoyed art class. The problem was I couldn't exactly tell what I liked about it. I couldn't put my feelings into words.

"Welllll....." I drew it out as I rearranged my sentences in my head. "I guess I liked learning about all the colors and stuff in art."

Mrs. Budd smiled. "I'm glad. I liked learning about art when I was your age, too."

She glanced behind her at the boys. "How was your day, guys?" she asked cheerily.

Two little eager voices talking over each other ensued.

"I got to do painting—"

"In Five in a Row we read this story about ducklings—"

"—and when I did gym with Mrs. Pete..."

"—and I really liked it, so could we get the book at the library this week?"

"...and MOM!..."

Thank goodness we soon pulled into a parking lot behind a large fenced-in field. Matthew and Titus sprung out of the car like two torpedoes just waiting to be launched and darted across the field to the play ground faster than a wink. I took my own sweet time, gracefully unbuckling my seat belt and stepping down from the car. Mrs. Budd must have noticed I wasn't as eager to be here as the boys, but she just smiled at me as she unloaded the cooler from the trunk.

"We'll go together," she said, and I fell into step beside her as we crossed the field.

As it turned out, there were more families at the park than I had banked on. I was about to despair— until I saw a girl in a green sweater swinging on the monkey bars, admired by a group of younger kids that stood nearby. It was Grace from science class!

I had not felt this feeling for so long; it almost seemed strange to me. I had nearly forgotten what it felt like to have a friend. Though I had only met Grace that morning, she was the closest anyone had ever come to being my friend. That normal feeling of excitement whenever you see someone; the happy anticipation of fun times ahead laughing and playing with a girl near your own age seemed so special to me. Others took these things as normal, everyday occurrences, but to me, it seemed above amazing.

Mrs. Budd dragged the lunch cooler over to a group of moms sitting at a wooden picnic table with their babies and toddlers. She nodded at me to go play, and called after me to come back when I got hungry.

I walked across the wood chips covering the play area, even attempting a little jog, as I made my way over to Grace, who was now sitting against a tree with a sandwich.

"Hey, Saranna!" she called as soon as she saw me approaching. She moved over and made room for me to sit next to her. I leaned my back against the rough bark of the tree and smiled at her.

"Hi! I didn't know you'd be here."

"I didn't know *you'd* be here," joked Grace, and I giggled.

A few moments of silence passed before I spoke. "I've never seen anything quite like this before."

"The playground?" questioned Grace, who looked puzzled out of her mind.

"Yeah," I sighed, almost under my breath.

Quickly recovering from her shock and pulling herself together again, she stuffed the rest of her sandwich into a plastic baggie and pushed herself off the ground, brushing the back of her capris as she did so.

"Well then, there's no better time to explore one than now. Come on!"

Before I could push myself off the ground, she grabbed my arm and pulled me up herself. Then she ran across the various apparatuses, with me doing my best to follow at her heels, duplicating her lightning quick patterns of ducking and jumping.

Ten minutes later, my stomach began to feel hollow, and I breathlessly suggested to Grace that we go sit by the picnic tables to eat the rest of our lunches.

I plopped myself down on the green grass, gasping as Mrs. Budd handed me a peanut butter and jelly sandwich. Grace realized that she had left the remains of her lunch under the tree, and ran back to get it. About 60 seconds later, a commotion erupted from that area of the park, and I looked up to see Grace chasing after a boy who was waving a plastic bag in his hand.

"Hey! That's my LUNCH, Mister!" shouted Grace as she ran after him, although her smile showed that she was anything but upset. "Some of us get hungry during the middle of a busy day, you know!" She joked as she followed the laughing boy under and over bridges, down slides, through tunnels and around kids and other obstacles.

Despite myself, I couldn't help laughing out loud at the scene. It was the first time I had laughed—like, really laughed—in ages. By the time Grace plopped down next to me, red faced and truly breathless, although holding her sandwich above her head triumphantly, she and I both collapsed into uncontrollable fits of laughter. We rolled over on the grass and just laughed and laughed. By the time we finally were able to look at each other seriously again, my cheeks felt like they were rubber bands and my eyes were moist with tears. We sat up and tried to eat our lunches, but every few bites, a couple giggles would escape one of us and set the other one off again.

After a little while, Matthew and Titus got hungry too, and brought their troop of young boys over to the picnic area to pick up their lunches. Grace and I decided that this was the opportune time to hang out on the playground, while all the others were busy eating.

I swung from monkey bar to monkey bar, my knuckles turning white from gripping the painted steel. By the time I made it across once, my hands felt sore and my arms seemed as if they had been stretched about three inches. Grace laughed and swung across easily and gracefully to meet me.

We trekked over to the sand pit to investigate the castles and dig sites the little boys had been working on. Grace showed me how to use a small bucket to make sand castles out of the wet sand at the bottom of the pit. I dug a moat around the architectural marvel and added a bridge for the dump trucks to drive over.

Next, we climbed under every tunnel and bridge until we found the most secure, hidden away cavity to talk in privacy. We talked about all kinds of things in the dampness of our fort: our classes at co-op, our favorite teachers so far, and our favorite colors. (Hers, not surprisingly, was green, while I was torn between purple and blue).

The playground began to get less and less busy as one family after another left to go home. Grace and I ventured out of our undercover hideaway after a group of boys with sticks pretending to be the "Patriots" capturing "Tories" busted in. That was okay. There were plenty of other places to hang out.

All too soon, it had to end. However, I left that playground excited at the prospect of future days like this one, and looking forward to next week when I could go to co-op again. I had a wonderful feeling deep in my heart. I felt *full.*

CHAPTER TEN

A couple weeks passed, and Grace had quickly become my best friend. Really, the only friend I had ever had! Once Mrs. Budd found out I loved to spend time with Grace, she set up times when we could hang out together, besides at co-op. I relished the special days when Grace could come over to the Budd's house and we would sit in my room for hours, giggling over magazines, listening to music on my IPod, and laughing at each other's silly stories. We both loved to read, and we often swapped books and then acted out our favorite parts in each. A couple times we even recruited Matthew and Titus to be a part of the scene, too! Sometimes we would get out some paints, paper, and colored pencils and I would show Grace the techniques I learned in art class each week. We would talk together, and I learned all about Grace and her family. It was on one of these days when Grace and I were both sitting on my bed, that Grace asked me one of her straight-forward, abrupt questions that completely shattered my peace.

"What happened before you were adopted?"

I froze. My whole body became tense and my brain started racing. How could she ask something like that?

"I lived in a group home," I said matter-of-factly, quickly recovering from my initial reaction.

"But how did you get there?" Grace persisted.

I turned and stared at her. She wanted the whole story? She had no idea what she was asking for.

"You know, most people don't try to pry old stories out of other people."

"Yeah, I know, but if we're going to be friends, we should know everything about each other, right?"

I begged to differ.

"And besides," she continued, a silly smile spreading across her face. "I'm not most people."

I gave a big, long, gusty sigh. I hoped that if I took long enough figuring out how to start, then she would eventually get bored waiting and change the subject. One full minute went by; two full minutes; three. Finally I realized that she wasn't going to give up. I sighed again before I started talking.

"I lived with my dad. I don't know what happened to my mom. I never knew her. I think she died while I was being born," I began. I stopped for a second. That was the easy part. My voice started taking on a far-away sound. "My dad seemed to love me...I don't know, really. He was taken to jail when I was seven."

"Why?" Grace asked. I looked in her face for the first time since I had started my story.

"I guess he was so desperate to provide for me that he took to stealing and gambling. The police caught on."

Here I stopped again, for a longer time than before. I was unearthing feelings that I had buried deep inside me for six years. Now, finally, they all began to surface. It was as if I were rediscovering my past. Digging down through piles and piles of old hurts and pains and getting to the deepest and the biggest ones. I continued: "They barged into our tiny little shack home in the dark, dismal neighborhood that we lived in with knives and guns. One grabbed me and held me from behind. The rest went after my father and pushed him against a wall. They handcuffed him and started to drag him away."

I closed my eyes. Tears were pouring down my cheeks. I felt like a knife was searing an infected wound; cutting deeper and deeper, until it began to dig out all the pus and infected flesh that was hindering me. "I was screaming and crying, fighting vigorously against the man who was gripping my arms behind me. I still remember the look on my daddy's face, as the police were pushing him farther and farther away from me. He was desperately calling my name..."

Even now, I could hear how his voice had sounded. My own voice choked and I stopped to listen. "Saranna! Saranna..." he had screamed. I could hear him, as clearly as if it were really happening. If I opened my eyes, I almost expected to find myself in the dark old shack again, surrounded by authorities who had no heart and didn't care about anything or anyone.

"I was taken to the police station. I sat there for hours as the police milled around making calls. I was angry. Angry at them for taking away my father and the only life I ever knew."

It felt surprisingly strange to admit that for the first time since I was seven. Yes, that was how I had felt. I was angry. And I realized that even now, I still was.

"What happened next?" Grace asked, breathlessly. Her eyes were wider than I had ever seen them before, and I realized that she was listening as if she were reliving my past with me. I reached for her hand.

"I ended up in two foster homes before I landed in the group home. The first foster home I was in, I was babied by the mother. I hated every moment of my life there. I ran away three weeks after my arrival."

"Wow," Grace commented.

"The second home I was in, the father drank and partied. My foster siblings were mad at me because they felt I took up too much of 'their' mom's time. They teased me constantly and even beat me up twice. Once the social workers found out about it, they took me out."

"Good thing they did," said Grace indignantly.

"Yeah," I whispered before going on.

"No one wanted me, so the authorities finally put me in a group home for foster kids." I shook my head fast and hard. I tried to dispel the images and memories that came to mind.

"I cannot describe how lonely, and dirty, and unhappy that place was. Everyone seemed like they were on automatic and there was no room for feelings. Every day was a dread and every night brought tears. I would hear children crying through the night, with no one there to comfort them through the long, dark hours."

Tears were streaming down my face again. I remembered listening to one little girl, who was maybe four. She would cry all night and her screams of "Mama! Mama!" would wake me up from a sound sleep. Her cries tore at my heart and even now came back to haunt me.

"That's where you learned to hide your feelings and bury your emotions," Grace said softly, looking not *at* me, but *through* me. The way she said it got me to think. And the more I thought about it, the more I saw how right she was. I had thought that since it was too painful for me to have emotions, I would just pretend that they weren't there. That way, I didn't have to feel the pain. And she was also right that I didn't just *do* it, I *learned* it. Gradually, after practicing, it became my lifestyle.

"I didn't have a choice," I said, feeling annoyance grow in my heart until it threatened to burst through my chest. My words came out sharp and curt. "I was protecting myself. Wasn't I right to do that? If I didn't, then...then..." My voice rose as I tried to figure out 'Then.' "...Then things would have been a whole lot worse than they already were!"

Grace nodded, and spoke in a loving, sweet way that immediately began shrinking the indignation that I felt. "I guess it was okay, but now when you don't tell the people who care about you how you feel, and you keep it all inside, you end up lying to yourself and not being able to differentiate your feelings and your actions. All that pent-up pain can grow and grow inside you until it bursts and starts poisoning your whole body. Sometimes it's good to be able to talk about things with others. It empties your heart out before it gets too full and over-crowded for God's love."

Her little speech made me think. Isn't that what had happened to me? I had let the hurt and pain grow and swell, pushing away all feelings of joy and peace— or, as she called it, 'God's love.' Had it really begun to poison my whole being, and blinded me from seeing any glimmer of hope?

Of course, now that I was finally relenting my brain kicked in and told me, *"No! You don't have to let go of all your feelings and put them out there for everyone to see and mock at! It's fine if you keep SOME of them in. It's a matter of privacy."*

I responded to Grace, "Look, I've just told you everything about me. Not even my adoptive parents know all of this. I know I can trust you, but I just want to know...you won't tell anyone, will you?"

Grace shook her head quickly. "No, I won't tell. I think you should be the one to tell your parents, anyway. They really do care about you. And they probably have been worrying about you, wanting to know what makes you the way you are. If you tell them, then they can help."

"I can't tell them!" I said, and then remembered to lower my voice. "I'm too confused. I would probably sound really silly in front of grown-ups. Do you really expect me to bring up the subject out of the blue?!"

"I'm sure they'd give you plenty of opportunities, so you wouldn't have to bring it up out of the blue," Grace said gently.

I opened my mouth for another rebuttal, but Grace interrupted me.

"It's okay; I don't want to argue with you, since I can understand how you're feeling. Trust me; there have been some things that I haven't wanted to tell my parents about for the longest time!"

Her voice got dead serious. "But if you are worried about feeling silly, then you can just tell God."

"What?"

"God cares about you even more than me, or your mom, or your dad, or even your other dad! He would want to know what's bothering you. And if you can confess your feelings to Him and ask His help to sort through them, then maybe you'll get more courage to tell your parents."

"Doesn't God already know all the things that have happened to me?" I countered, not able to keep the sarcasm out of my voice.

"Sure, but He'd still like to hear it from you. It's more to help you than to help Him."

"How's that," I said roughly.

"Because it's just like if you were to tell me or your parents. It would make you feel better because you wouldn't be so alone with all the hurt and pain locked up inside. And God would NEVER think of you as silly or dumb! He knows you, He made you, and He understands what you've been through, because He's been through it all with you."

I sat and thought about this for a good long while. The clock ticked in the background. Every footstep from the house echoed in our ears. My brain was working so hard it was starting to hurt. I rubbed my temples.

"Okay, okay, I'll think about it later. My brain already hurts."

"Alright." Grace smiled at me and squeezed my hand. "Thank you for trusting me enough to share with me," she whispered.

CHAPTER ELEVEN

Three weeks went by since my talk with Grace. She didn't mention anything else about it, which was good, because if she had I probably would have clobbered her. In fact, she acted as if it hadn't even happened. I was sort of glad. I needed to be left alone with my feelings. But wait! There I went again, trying to hide everything deep in my heart. I got so frustrated with myself that I couldn't even imagine talking to my adoptive parents about it. I couldn't bring myself to talk to God about it, either... if He even existed in the first place. Something in my mind kept telling me, *"This is silly! Don't even bother; it won't help."*

Even as my soul was in turmoil, I could still ignore it sometimes. It seemed like my brain got so tired of thinking that it stopped altogether. That was fine with me! I stayed busy with my new family, learning new things and meeting new people and visiting new places. Co-op continued on through the winter, and then it was April. We stopped meeting regularly at the church, but we still kept in touch with some of the people we had gotten to know better. Sometimes we would go to a park with them, visit their homes or invite them to ours, or someone would organize a field trip and invite the whole home school group to go. At first all the new people had been intimidating to me, but as I gradually became adjusted I began enjoying both meeting at co-op and meeting outside of co-op. After I had gotten used to everyone, I enjoyed visiting in an organized environment. I discovered that I loved to learn things, and learning in a group setting turned out to be a fun addition to learning on my own. It was also pretty exciting when we would come together spontaneously and just enjoy some light-hearted fun. I especially liked it when the Budds invited whole families over to their house or when we would all go over to another family's house.

One Wednesday morning, Mrs. Budd surprised me by saying that Grace's family was arranging a picnic at the park. I felt something in my stomach leap up to my throat as I bounced on my toes in excited anticipation.

"When do we leave?" I asked.

"In a few hours," she answered, laughing to see me so excited about something.

You'd better believe I ran around like a bee who had just found a whole field of flowers in order to get us all ready to leave on time!

Once we got to the park, I didn't hang back behind Mrs. Budd like I had the first time. This time, I ran ahead with the boys, spotting Grace one hundred yards away. She saw me too, and ran to meet me with the same enthusiasm.

"Yeah!!" we laughed and shouted as we swung each other around in circles.

As I took off to play with Grace, I felt a strange kind of happiness to be in the same place that our friendship together had begun so many months before. It felt weird to think of how much I had grown and changed in even that short amount of time.

We joked and ran and played just like we had before, except there was a new kind of element now. We were friends, true friends.

After about an hour, Grace asked, "Which structure do you think is your favorite?"

I thought a little while, then pointed to a large wooden one that had many different bridges, ladders, and tunnels leading up to a main cathedral like fort that towered high above the rest of the playground.

"I like that one, too," confided Grace. "It would make a really great building for a secret agent place, with all those different exits and entrances. And that ladder made out of tires looks like a huge bulwark."

"Let's go!" I said, leading the way up a ramp to a covered bridge, up a short ladder, and across a bridge of boards linked together all the way up the cathedral fort. Grace followed.

Sitting cross legged on the wood planks of the fort, Grace and I seemed to run out of things to say. After a few moments of silence, Grace asked, "Saranna, are you a Christian?"

She didn't blurt it out—she said it in all sincerity. Yet I seemed to lose any sense of security I had ever had before.

Was I a Christian? I had absolutely no idea. I suppose I sat on the fence when it came to religion. I mean, I had been to church off and on for almost my whole life. The family who had adopted me, whom I apparently now found my identity in, was obviously devoutly religious. But where did I stand? Did the Budds' religion automatically encompass me? Could I have no religion at all?

The subject seemed to weigh on me. With each passing day the burden became darker and heavier. With each passing moment, the urge to talk to Mr. or Mrs. Budd became stronger and stronger. Whenever I was around them, I felt like blurting out the question to them. I pictured how it would look: I would suddenly, out of nowhere, blurt out, "Am I a Christian?" I'd probably shock them enough that they would *have* to tell me the truth! But each chance that presented itself silently slipped away from my grasp. Either one of the little boys would "conveniently" burst into the room with an urgent need, or the grown-ups would excuse themselves to go and finish a chore or work project that they were in the middle of. Or sometimes, I would just plain chicken out. *"No, now is not a good time; I don't feel ready,"* I would tell myself. Or, *"What if they think I'm crazy and too irreligious for them? Would they shun me or treat me differently?"* And the most terrifying thought of all: *"What if THEY don't know the answer?"* If they didn't know, then how would I ever find the true answer to this ever burning question?

The thoughts and worries made my head spin, so that whenever I was alone with Mr. or Mrs. Budd, I felt dizzy and lightheaded enough that I knew I'd sound like a lunatic bringing up the subject then.

After about 2 weeks, I still had not worked up the guts to ask. I couldn't sleep well during the night for all my thinking and tossing and turning. Try as I might, I could not figure out the answer to my own question—I only became more confused. It appeared more and more obvious that I HAD to talk to Mr. and Mrs. Budd about it. Sometimes, during the day, I would catch Mrs. Budd studying me when she thought I was absorbed in some reading material or an art project. In reality, my eyes were staring at a blank sheet in front of me, and my brain was doing the whirling and spinning charade all over again.

Then one day...

"Saranna," Mr. Budd's voice called me as I passed his office. I peeked in and saw that he sat in the computer chair while Mrs. Budd leaned against the desk next to him.

"Yes?"

"Are you busy right now?" he asked me.

"Well..." I stopped. I was going to tell him that I was headed to my room to get some schoolwork done, but actually, I was just walking around with no real purpose except that I can think better when I'm moving. "No," I finally settled on as my answer.

"Why don't you come on in, then," he motioned to me.

Oh no. In that instant I recognized that either he or Mrs. Budd knew something about what had been bugging me. Why else would they both want to talk to me privately? Or was it something more serious that was happening? What if...? I felt a surge of fear prick my stomach. I willfully made my feet move themselves slowly into the room, and stiffly leaned up against the desk next to Mrs. Budd. She put her arm around me, and looked to her husband to say something next.

"You know, we've noticed that sometimes you seem a bit...withdrawn. We realize that this transition has been really hard on you, and we just want you to know that we care about you, and even though it might be hard, we want you to feel comfortable talking to us about how you feel," he started.

I began to feel pretty *un*comfortable.

"Even though it's a lot to adjust to, we hope that eventually you'll be able to feel like a part of our family, because in our hearts, you have already become a member of our family. And families need to be able to communicate with each other, no matter how hard it is."

I looked down at the floor and nodded. I knew where he was taking this.

"I guess you want me to tell you everything that's going on with me, then?" I whispered.

Mr. Budd looked at me and didn't say anything for a moment or two. "Yes," he finally answered, just as softly. "We're worried about you and want to be able to help you deal with whatever feelings are hurting you. We know something has been bothering you lately."

I sighed. I wasn't sure if I was ready for this. Should I tell them everything? What did I have to lose? But then again, what if they didn't understand? I began to feel dizzy.

CHAPTER TWELVE

⁶⁶Hey," Mrs. Budd said gently, peering into my eyes. "This is what we're here for. A family is there for you when you need support, and it's a parent's job to be there especially for their kids."

I raised my eyes to just barely meet hers. "How come you can always see right through me?" I complained out loud.

Mr. Budd laughed and Mrs. Budd grinned, trying not to laugh as well. "I guess that's just one of the tools that God gave to us to help us understand our kids when they aren't brave enough to share it with us themselves," she said lovingly.

Ouch. She sure hit the nail on the head with that one. Still, I hesitated.

"It's okay, Saranna, you can tell us what's wrong," Mr. Budd coaxed gently.

"We won't think any differently of you," added Mrs. Budd. "Nothing could ever change how much we love you."

My eyes traced the pattern of the rug even as they filled with tears. Now I realized it. These were people who really, truly cared about me. More than I ever would know, they loved me. And they were willing to take the time and energy to express that love for me and listen to whatever messy troubles I was dealing with right then that could easily have been dismissed as 'my problem.'

I caved. I decided to tell them everything. Yes, everything; but where to begin? I groped for words to explain my mixed up, messed up, glob of feelings that were buried in my heart beneath all the hurt and anger that had stayed with me since I was little.

"It's just..." And then the tears started flowing. I cried in jagged breaths as I tried to talk through my distress.

"I don't know who I am anymore! I don't know who I belong to! And I don't know why I'm supposed to be here! I thought I was my birth father's, but then he had to go get put in jail, so I belonged to first one family, then another, then I was dumped in a group home. Now, I'm told I belong to you, even though I don't know you and can hardly fit in here at all. I can't...I can't figure out if I'm French, or American, or if I'm a Christian, or...or...something else. And I can't figure out what to do with myself!"

All throughout my rant, Mr. and Mrs. Budd just listened intently, worry lines creasing their brows. Now that I was done, I was crying too hard to notice that they were on the verge of crying themselves. Through a blur of tears I found Mrs. Budd's outstretched arms and fell into them, crumpled in a heap of helplessness and emptiness. Tears ran down my face in a steady stream, and my nose dripped so that I kept having to sniffle loudly. I cried so hard that my stomach started hurting. Mr. Budd stood up, walked over to us, and put his comforting hand on my back as I sobbed and sobbed. All the pain came out and I couldn't hide it this time; all the pain from my childhood, from the foster families, from my orphanage, and from all my shattered dreams.

When I finally quieted down enough to think straight, Mr. Budd started explaining.

"I'm sorry, Saranna. As you describe it, I can understand how you feel. I think everyone can, to some degree or another, because at some time in their life, they have to face those tough questions like, 'Who am I? And why am I here?' Sometimes you only have to answer them once, but sometimes, you have to face the same question multiple times. But everyone has to face it sometime or another. Thankfully—" and here he reached across his desk and picked up his Bible from on top of a pile of papers, "—this book tells us the answer to those questions."

"It does?" I asked, sniffling once more and wiping my nose on my shirt sleeve.

"Yes," Mr. Budd answered, sitting down in his big computer chair. "Would you like to read a few passages with me?" he asked and beckoned me over.

Though my breath was still coming in jagged spurts that made it difficult to talk, I nodded and walked over to him. Mr. Budd put his arm around my shoulders and sat me down right next to him. Then he opened his Bible.

"First you need to understand about what life was like in the very beginning. God created man to be in fellowship with Him, to walk with Him, to talk with Him, and to draw all of his life from Him. In fact, God was the one who brought man to life. In the first book of the Bible, God tells us how He did that: He breathed the breath of life into his nostrils."

"God gave man a choice—he could either live in God's perfect will and have life, or he could live in his own will and have death. Man chose to be a slave to himself, instead of being a servant to God. Ever since we, as human beings, made that decision, there has been an un-crossable gap between us and God. The gap was our sin. God is perfect and cannot be around sin. That's why when we chose to disobey God, we had to become separated from Him forever. AND, since God is the one who gives us the breath of life, we would die apart from Him."

Here Mr. Budd paused and asked me, "Are you understanding so far?"

I nodded, processing as he was talking.

Mrs. Budd picked up where he had left off. "Satan, who is the devil, became our master when we decided to disobey God. Now, we would always be a slave to our sinful desires and have the conflict between our will and God's. God set up the world so that there ALWAYS has to be a punishment for sin."

"But, what if it's only a *small* sin?" I countered, thinking of all the times I had done bad things in my whole life.

"It doesn't matter," Mrs. Budd shook her head. "No matter how small your sin is God still has to punish you for it. And the punishment is the same for all sins: Eternal separation from God. In other words, we are all sentenced to hell."

I had begun to feel scared. As horrible as I thought my life was, I didn't want to die yet. I had never thought of life after death, and wasn't even sure if there was a life after death. But the death that Mrs. Budd was describing sounded awful. I looked to Mr. Budd for reassurance, but he was nodding, agreeing with everything Mrs. Budd was saying.

"Isn't God really...cruel to punish everyone that severely? Because I'm sure that everyone in the world has disobeyed His commandments at some time or another."

Mrs. Budd answered. "You are right that everyone has disobeyed God's commandments. Nobody could ever live up to His perfect standard, except God himself. But it's not God's cruelty that punishes us; it's His goodness."

"Huhhh?!?"

"If God is perfectly good and just, then He can't turn a blind eye to wrongdoing. If a police officer or a judge did that, he would be a bad judge, because a good judge *has* to punish evil doers," reasoned Mr. Budd.

"But, even from the beginning of time, God had a plan to redeem us," Mrs. Budd interjected, motioning to Mr. Budd.

Mr. Budd then began to read from his Bible. "'For God so loved the world, that He sent His one and only Son, that whosoever believes in Him, shall not perish, but have everlasting life.'"[2]

Mr. Budd looked up. I slowly let the words sink into my heart. I turned them over and over in my head, drawing pleasure from the sound and meaning of them. I looked to Mr. Budd to explain further.

"You see," he said, "the punishment for our sin HAD to be paid. But God knew that we couldn't pay a price that large, no matter how hard we tried. However, there was only one other way for it to be paid."

I offered a confused expression. "What was that?"

"A perfect sacrifice had to be made. Someone who had lived an absolutely perfect life had to pay the awful price for our sin, so that we could be set free."

"But...I thought you said no one was perfect." Even as I said that, the answer dawned on me. "God...?" I said breathlessly.

Mrs. Budd nodded. "God had to do it for us, because we couldn't do it ourselves. We had a terrible price to pay for our sins, but God paid that price for us."

---

[2] John 3:16

Mr. Budd flipped through the pages of his Bible until he came to the place he was looking for. "Isaiah 53 explains how God redeemed us much better than I can:

Surely He has borne our griefs and carried our sorrows; yet we esteemed Him stricken, smitten by God, and afflicted. But He was wounded for our transgressions; He was crushed for our iniquities; upon Him was the chastisement that brought us peace, and with His stripes we are healed."

I felt a lump of frustration rise in my throat. "I don't understand all those fancy words!" I cried.

Mrs. Budd leaned over and pointed to the words as she explained. "When Jesus died on the cross, He was being *wounded* for our sins. He was being *crushed* for our wrongdoing. He *carried* the punishment, so that we could have peace. By His wounds, by the *stripes* that He bore on his body from the brutal whipping, we are healed from our terrible illness that doesn't just bring death, but *eternal* death. It is called sin."

She looked up and finished with a word of finality. "Jesus bridged the gap between us and God."

CHAPTER THIRTEEN

I let the words sink in. I felt even more over-whelmed than I had when I finally figured out that Mr. and Mrs. Budd really loved me more than I would ever know. And now, as they had taken the time to explain to me exactly what God had done for us, I felt an even greater weight of gratitude settle on my heart. Yet I wasn't sure I was ready to receive this great gift. I didn't deserve it! The humility that came from the knowledge of my unworthiness for God's grace encompassed me.

I saw Mr. and Mrs. Budd were thinking the same thing. I was hearing this for the first time, but although they had doubtlessly heard it many times over, as they gazed at each other, I could see the same sense of awe I was feeling pass between them.

Mr. Budd seemed to speak from a well of grat-itude to God that both of their hearts shared. "'For one will scarcely die for a righteous person—though perhaps for a good person one would dare even to die—but God shows His love for us in that while we were still sinners, Christ died for us.'"[3]

The moment seemed too divine, too fragile to interrupt. Could this really be true? It seemed almost too grand to even hope to be true. I sat soaking it in, silently crying out my thanks to God for His mercy on me. A part of me had no idea what to say to a God that must be great and awesome beyond my imagination, but another part of me just seemed to automatically know how to speak to God, even though I had never seen Him in person...until now. I didn't have to see God with my physical eyes in order to see Him with my heart. I could see and feel His love so clearly that I knew He must be real.

"But that is not all!" Mrs. Budd abruptly exclaimed, as if she had forgotten the best part of the story. "Clark, read Romans 8:15-17."

Mr. Budd smiled as he flipped through the thin pages, finding the right place.

"For you did not receive the spirit of slavery to fall back into fear, but you have received the Spirit of adoption as sons, by whom we cry, 'Abba! Father!' The Spirit himself bears witness with our spirit that we are children of God, and if children, then heirs— heirs of God and fellow heirs with Christ...'"

"Do you see?" Mrs. Budd asked. "Because Jesus redeemed us—bought us back from our sinfulness that held us in bondage—God gave us the free gift of eternal life in Heaven with Him. He adopted ALL

---

[3] Romans 5:6-8

of us as His children again!" She held me by the shoulders and stood face to face with me. "Saranna, He wants to give you the gift! He has a treasure that is just waiting for you! All you have to do is accept it."

I sat back, stunned by what she said.

"Saranna," she continued in a soft voice, which sounded as if it held the answer to the greatest mystery. "It doesn't matter who you 'belong to' on this earth. If you belong to Him, no one can take His gift away from you, after you accept it. HE is your *real* Father."

Something in my mind clicked. This is what I had been missing! If I accepted God's free gift, then I could be anywhere, in any circumstance, and under anyone's care, but I would still be the same person, because who I am would not be *completely* dictated by my relation to this world. I was born to my father, and I loved him. I was adopted by Mr. Budd, and he loved me. But even more important than the love of my earthly fathers, was the love that I would receive as God's child. He loved me so much that He died for me so that I could go to Heaven with Him. I was an heir to His treasure of everlasting life! Now, I began to fit together all the puzzle pieces. I was finally understanding how to be loyal to both of my fathers. I could still love them just the same, even though I didn't live with one of them anymore. I could do that because I had been given the eternal love of my Heavenly Father. On earth, it mattered who my father was. But in Heaven, the only father's love I would ever need was God's.

Even before I had come to America, I knew innately that I needed to make a choice, but I felt lost because I didn't know which way to look. Now I knew what I was going to choose. I wanted the eternal gift of God's love. I turned to Mrs. Budd.

"Thank you...Mom" I whispered as I hugged her with all my might. I buried my face in her shoulder, so I could barely hear myself utter the last word, but she heard it. Through her tears, she hugged me back just as hard, and pressed her lips up against my head. "I love you more than you'll ever know," she told me empathetically. Then I turned to him. "And thank you, Daddy." I said it quickly, before I had time to think about it, but I had said it. I had said it.

He held out his arms to me and before I knew it I was in them, being smothered by the love of a father who truly cared for me. "I'm so blessed to have you as my daughter," he told me.

I pulled away and looked into his eyes. They brimmed with tears of joy and I said what I wanted to say not just because I had to, not just because it felt like the right thing to say at the moment, but because I really meant it in my heart. "I love you, Daddy."

EPILOGUE

I walked back from the ticket counter to my family, who were waiting with me at the airport. Mom held me in the same way she did when I had first arrived in America, feeling cast off and lonely.

"My big 19-year old," she whispered.

I wrapped my arms around her. Tears fell on her shoulder again. This time, tears of happiness. I remembered vividly that miraculous day in June when I had first met my family at this very airport. As I now stood there in my mother's arms, I reflected on what had taken place in the last six years. God's fingerprints were all over my life.

And now I was going back. I was going to find my father in France. I had discussed this at length with Mom and Dad, and they felt that I was ready. I had it in my heart that if I found my father, I would tell him about Jesus, the God in whom I had found refuge. I wanted to see my dad in Heaven. I wanted him to experience the joy and the freedom that Christ had given me. This time, though, I didn't imagine our greeting as a happy ending to a fairy tale, as I had so many years ago. No, this time it would be different. I didn't know what to expect, but I knew that it was God's will for me to go. Maybe my father wouldn't even recognize me. Maybe I wouldn't ever find him. Even though doubts tempted to plague my mind, I felt a peace in my heart that could only come from the presence of God. He wanted me to go and share my story and Jesus' message with others in my native country. And I was ready. By God's grace, I was prepared. It was no mental readiness, but more of a readiness of heart. I knew that I could not do this on my own strength. Even though my heart was prepared, I had to rest on the Almighty's strength to bring me through. "'The spirit is willing, but the flesh is weak.'"[4] Mom had given this verse to me to memorize when I first spoke to her about my desires.

This is my story, but this is His message. Maybe you don't know the assurance of Heaven that I do because of His forgiveness. I pray that someday soon you will understand His perfect plan of redemption. I know that I will always be inadequate to receive His gift, but that's the whole reason that Jesus went to the cross. What greater picture of love can there be? No matter who you are, or where you are in your life right now, know that God is real and that Jesus loves you. It doesn't matter if others reject you on this earth because Jesus will embrace you. And

---

[4] Matthew 26:41b

there is no better feeling than falling into the open arms of our Redeemer.

Now that I am a Christian, I know who I really am. I am chosen, I am clean, and I belong to God; I am His workmanship. I have Jesus' righteousness; I have been justified, and I am set free from sin. I am called to be a saint. I am reconciled, I am forgiven, I am His daughter, and therefore an heir to His gift of salvation. I am blessed; I have been delivered from the domain of darkness and raised from death in my sins. I can now boldly access God in prayer because of Jesus Christ. Even though I may feel weary and burdened, I am loved, because I have been shown grace and mercy in countless ways. I am sealed for all eternity; I am merely a sojourner and exile in this world, because I share in a Heavenly calling, and am a partaker in the promise. If you have claimed Christ's suffering on your behalf, and God's promise to give you eternal life, then you are all these things, too.

You are His Princess. And your Father loves you.

ENDNOTES:

If you would like to read more from God's word about what it means to be His Child, here are some of my favorite passages:

John 1:12, John 3:3-6, John 15:1-5 and 15-16, Romans 5:1, Romans 6:17-18, Romans 8, 2 Corinthians 1:21-22, Galatians 3:26-28, Galatians 4:6-7, Ephesians 1:3-8, Ephesians 2:4-10 and 19, Colossians 1:13-14, Hebrews 3:1 and 14-15, Hebrews 4: 14-16, 1 Peter 2:9-12, Revelation 5:9-10.

CPSIA information can be obtained
at www.ICGtesting.com
Printed in the USA
FSHW011327230119
55210FS

9 781498 415033